Stories of the Christmas Elves

Elyse V.K. Burns-Hill

Stories of the Christmas Elves

ISBN: 9798871359617

Edition 1 Published December 2023

Printed By Amazon Publishing Services in the UK

Published by Millabelle Publishing
c/o ElyseBH Consulting Ltd
Hursley Park Road
Winchester
Hampshire
SO21 2JN

For Izzy and Milly

Merry Christmas, my loves; I hope you enjoy these stories about the Christmas Elves.

You chose for all profits for this book to go to the NSPCC to help look after the children; I will make sure that happens.

Lots of love
Mummy xx

Stories of the Christmas Elves

Contents

The Night the Sleigh Stood Still

Reading Time: 12m

In the frost-kissed realm of the North Pole, where snowflakes danced like tiny stars and the northern lights painted the sky in vibrant hues, there was a place brimming with joy and laughter known to all as Santa's Workshop. Here, nestled among glittering icicles and candy cane trees, a group of cheerful elves lived and worked, their hearts full of the magic of Christmas.

Among these elves was a little one named Elara. Elara was not like the other elves. She was smaller, with twinkling emerald eyes and ears that curved just a little bit more than usual. She often found herself lost in her own world, dreaming up inventions and ideas that were quite unusual for an elf.

Each day, as Christmas drew nearer, the workshop buzzed with excitement. Elves in colourful hats and aprons scurried about, crafting toys, wrapping gifts, and humming merry tunes. Jingles of bells and the sweet scent of gingerbread filled the air as everyone prepared for the most wonderful night of the year.

But this year, something extraordinary was about to happen, something that would need more than just the usual elvish merriment and magic. It was a challenge that would require the unique talents of an elf who dared to think differently. And little did Elara know, she was just the elf for the job.

As the northern sky shimmered with auroras, a problem arose that sent a wave of worry through Santa's Workshop. The heart of Christmas, Santa's magical sleigh, which had always glowed with a warm, enchanting light, had suddenly dimmed and grown silent. The elves gathered around it, their faces a mix of concern and confusion.

"The sleigh's magic is fading!" exclaimed Tinsel, the head elf, his voice echoing through the workshop. "Without it, we can't deliver the presents on Christmas Eve!"

The elves buzzed with anxious chatter. This had never happened before. The sleigh, crafted from the rarest winter woods and enchanted by the most powerful of Christmas spells, was the key to their Christmas Eve journey. Without its magic, the spirit of Christmas was at risk.

In the midst of the commotion, Elara stood quietly at the back, her mind racing. She noticed something unusual about the sleigh, something the others hadn't seen. But Elara, often lost in her inventive thoughts and quirky ideas, hesitated. She wondered if her different way of seeing things could really help in such a serious situation.

Meanwhile, the other elves were trying everything they knew. They sprinkled extra fairy dust, chanted ancient elvish incantations, and even attempted to jump-start the sleigh with the power of their jolliest laughs. But nothing worked. The sleigh remained dull and lifeless, its magic seemingly drained.

As hope began to dwindle, Elara's heart pounded with a mixture of fear and excitement. She realised that this might be the moment to share her unique idea, no matter how unconventional it might seem. It was a risk, but with Christmas at stake, it was one she knew she had to take.

Elara, gathering her courage, stepped forward. "I have an idea," she said, her voice barely above a whisper, but it carried in the silent workshop. All eyes turned to her.

Elara explained her observation: the sleigh's magic didn't just come from spells and fairy dust; the joy and belief of children around the world powered it. "What if," she proposed, "we find a way to rekindle that joy and belief to recharge the sleigh?"

The elves exchanged puzzled glances. This was a concept they hadn't considered. It wasn't the traditional elvish way of fixing things. But with no other options, Tinsel nodded. "Let's try Elara's idea," he declared.

Elara, with the help of her fellow elves, set to work. They crafted a special device – a Joyometer – designed to capture and measure the joy and belief from children's letters to Santa. The plan was to use these powerful emotions to reignite the sleigh's magic.

As the elves began sorting through the mountains of letters, they were touched by the heartfelt wishes and the pure belief in the magic of Christmas. Each letter, filled with love and hope, made the Joyometer glow brighter.

Meanwhile, Elara faced her own set of challenges. She had to fine-tune the Joyometer to ensure it could channel the collected joy and belief into the sleigh. It was a task that required precision and imagination, qualities that Elara had in abundance.

Night after night, as the Northern Lights danced above, Elara worked tirelessly, adjusting gears and recalibrating dials. The other elves supported her, inspired by her determination and innovative approach.

Finally, as the Joyometer brimmed with the magic of children's joy and belief, it was time to test it on the sleigh. The elves gathered, holding their breath as Elara connected the device to the heart of the sleigh.

At first, nothing happened, and a wave of disappointment swept through the workshop. But then, slowly, a faint twinkle appeared on the sleigh. It was working!

The faint twinkle on the sleigh grew steadily, casting a warm, golden glow around the workshop. The elves cheered, but Elara knew the hardest part was yet to come. To fully restore the sleigh's magic, they needed to channel the joy and belief directly from the Joyometer into its core.

With a deep breath, Elara started the transfer process. The workshop was filled with a tense silence, broken only by the humming of the Joyometer. Slowly, the sleigh began to absorb the joyful energy, its colours becoming brighter, its magic stronger.

But then, unexpectedly, the Joyometer started to flicker and buzz. It was overloading! The immense power of the children's belief was more than Elara had anticipated. The sleigh's lights began to flicker in response, threatening to go out again.

Realising the danger, Elara acted quickly. She adjusted the connections, redistributing the energy flow. Her hands moved with precision and confidence, guided by her unique understanding of the magical and the mechanical.

The other elves watched, awestruck by her skill and bravery. Tinsel, the head elf, realised that Elara's different way of thinking was exactly what they had needed all along. Her innovative approach and quick thinking were saving Christmas.

With one final adjustment, Elara stabilised the Joyometer. The sleigh responded, its lights shining steadily once more.

The magic was back, stronger than ever, fueled by the pure joy and belief of children from all over the world.

The workshop erupted into cheers and applause. Elara, panting and smiling, stepped back. The sleigh, now fully recharged, glowed with a brilliant light, ready to embark on its Christmas journey.

Santa, who had been watching from a distance, came forward with a wide smile. "Elara," he said, "you've done it! You've saved Christmas!"

The atmosphere in Santa's Workshop was now one of jubilation and relief. Elves hugged each other, laughing and cheering, their eyes shining with pride and happiness. They gathered around Elara, lifting her onto their shoulders as a hero.

Santa, with a twinkle in his eye, thanked Elara and her team for their remarkable work. "Your unique perspective and brave heart have reminded us all of the true spirit of Christmas," he said. "It's not just about the magic we have, but about the magic we create together."

With the sleigh's magic restored, the elves quickly resumed their work, more energised than ever. They loaded the sleigh with beautifully wrapped gifts, each one crafted with love and care.

Elara watched, her heart full. She had overcome her doubts and fears, proving to herself and everyone else that being different was not just okay; it was important. Her ideas, once hidden in the shadows of her thoughts, had now saved Christmas.

The night of Christmas Eve arrived. Santa, in his red suit and jolly hat, climbed into the gleaming sleigh, now ready for its magical journey. The reindeer, sensing the excitement, pranced and pawed, eager to take flight.

As Santa prepared to depart, he gave a special nod to Elara. "Remember," he said, "every one of you is vital to the magic of Christmas. Elara's courage to share her unique gifts has made this night possible."

With a hearty "Ho Ho Ho," Santa took the reins, and the sleigh lifted off into the starry night. The elves cheered, watching as the sleigh soared into the sky, its trail of magic lighting up the dark.

Elara stood among her friends, her heart swelling with joy and pride. She had not only saved Christmas but had also found her own place in the world of elves, a place where her differences were celebrated and valued.

As the night wore on, the North Pole settled into a peaceful silence. The elves, after a long and eventful day, gathered in the warmth of the workshop, sharing stories and sipping hot cocoa.

Elara, surrounded by her fellow elves, felt a deep sense of belonging. She had learned that her unique ideas were not just quirks but gifts to be shared. And the other elves learned from Elara too, understanding that every elf, no matter how different, had something special to contribute.

Outside, the sky shimmered with the Northern Lights, reflecting the joy and magic of the world below. The elves knew that Santa was out there, spreading happiness and gifts, all thanks to their teamwork and Elara's bravery.

As the first light of dawn touched the snowy peaks of the North Pole, the elves made their way to their cosy beds, their hearts full of the joy and wonder of Christmas.

And so, the story of how Elara and her unique idea saved Christmas became a cherished tale in Santa's Workshop. It was a story told every year, a reminder that the true magic of Christmas lies in believing in oneself and embracing the differences that make each of us special.

The End

The Elves' Midnight Mission

Reading Time: 17m

In the heart of the wintery North Pole, where snowflakes danced like tiny ballerinas and the night sky glowed with a million stars, stood the most magical place on Earth – Santa's Workshop. This bustling haven of Christmas cheer was home to Santa's team of diligent elves, each working tirelessly to ensure a perfect Christmas for children all around the world.

Among these elves were two special friends, Jinx and Jolly. Jinx, with her neatly tied hair and glasses perched on her nose, was the epitome of precision and order. Her methodical approach to toy-making was legendary. Next to her, always in a whirl of energy and laughter, was Jolly. His bright eyes and untamed curls mirrored his creative and sometimes chaotic way of working.

As Christmas Eve approached, the workshop was a flurry of activity. Elves wrapped presents with ribbons and bows, the scent of gingerbread wafted through the air, and the sound of jingling bells filled the workshop. Santa, with his hearty laugh and kind eyes, oversaw the preparations, his heart swelling with pride at his team's hard work.

But in the midst of this festive hustle and bustle, an oversight occurred. A small batch of very special toys, destined for children who had written the most heartfelt letters to Santa, sat unfinished in a corner of the workshop. These were not just any toys; they were crafted with extra care and love, meant to bring joy to those who needed it most.

As the clock ticked closer to midnight, the time when Santa would depart on his sleigh, Jinx and Jolly stumbled upon the forgotten toys. A wave of worry washed over them. Could they finish these toys in time without Santa or the other elves noticing?

Determined to save Christmas for these special children, Jinx and Jolly embarked on a secret mission, a mission that would test their friendship, their skills, and their spirit of Christmas.

Under the soft glow of moonlight filtering through the workshop windows, Jinx and Jolly stood in front of the unfinished toys, their hearts racing. They both knew what they had to do, but the task was daunting. With Santa's departure only hours away, they had a narrow window of time to complete these special toys.

"We can't let these children down," Jinx said determinedly, her eyes scanning the workshop for tools and materials they would need.

Jolly nodded in agreement, his usual jovial face now etched with concern. "But we need to be quick and quiet," he whispered. "If Santa finds out, he'll think we don't trust him to fix it. And we can't worry the other elves!"

Their mission was clear: secretly finishing the toys without alerting Santa or the other elves. It was a task that required stealth, speed, and a whole lot of elvish ingenuity.

Jinx, ever the planner, quickly devised a strategy. "We'll divide and conquer," she suggested. "I'll work on assembling the parts, and you can paint and decorate."

Jolly, however, was more concerned about the logistics of their covert operation. "But what about the noise? And how will we get all the materials without being noticed?"

The two friends pondered the challenges ahead. The workshop was still bustling with elves wrapping gifts, checking lists, and tending to the reindeer. Any unusual activity could raise suspicion.

Despite these obstacles, Jinx and Jolly's resolve only strengthened. They knew that the true spirit of Christmas was about bringing joy, and they couldn't bear the thought of even one child waking up to an incomplete Christmas.
As the workshop clock chimed, marking the hours slipping away, Jinx and Jolly began their secret mission. With a shared look of determination, they stepped into the shadows, ready

to do whatever it took to ensure every child would have a magical Christmas morning.

As the North Pole clock continued its steady march towards midnight, Jinx and Jolly embarked on their daring task. They moved stealthily around the workshop, gathering materials for the unfinished toys. Jinx carefully selected gears and tiny screws while Jolly scooped up glitter and colourful paint pots. They communicated with subtle gestures and whispers, trying not to draw any attention.

In a quiet corner of the workshop, they set up a secret workstation shielded by stacks of gift boxes. Jinx meticulously assembled the toy parts, her fingers moving with practised precision. Jolly, with his artistic flair, brought the toys to life with vibrant colours and sparkling decorations. Their contrasting styles complemented each other, Jinx's attention to detail and Jolly's creative touch working in harmony.

However, the task was not without its challenges. At one point, Jolly accidentally knocked over a jar of glitter, sending a sparkling cloud into the air. They froze, hearts pounding, but luckily, the other elves were too engrossed in their tasks to notice.

Time seemed to fly as they worked, and the midnight deadline loomed ever closer. They encountered another hurdle when they realised they were short on a specific type of paint needed for the final toy. Jolly's eyes widened in panic, but Jinx calmed him down. "I'll sneak over to the supply room and grab what we need," she said, slipping away like a shadow.

Meanwhile, Jolly worked double-time, adding the finishing touches to the other toys. His hands were a blur of motion, painting and decorating with a speed he never knew he had.

Just when Jinx returned with the paint, the unexpected happened. Santa, making his final rounds before his journey, began to approach their hidden corner. Jinx and Jolly's hearts sank. If Santa discovered them now, their mission would be over.

In a split-second decision, Jolly created a diversion. He set off a small, noisy toy car, drawing Santa's attention away from their secret workshop. Santa chuckled at the playful toy, unaware of the real drama unfolding just meters away.

With Santa diverted, Jinx and Jolly quickly completed the final toy, a beautiful miniature sleigh with reindeer, just as the clock struck its ominous toll: midnight.

The midnight chime echoed through Santa's Workshop, signalling the moment of Santa's departure. Jinx and Jolly, with the completed toys in their arms, exchanged a glance of mixed panic and determination. They had one final, crucial task: to place the toys into Santa's sack without being noticed.

As Santa, with his bag almost ready, turned his back to attend to a last-minute detail from Mrs. Claus, Jinx and Jolly seized their moment. Moving with the utmost care, they tiptoed towards the towering sack of presents. Their hearts raced, knowing that the success of their entire mission hung in the balance.

Just as they were about to place the toys into the sack, the unthinkable happened. A loose floorboard under Jolly's foot creaked loudly, cutting through the silence of the workshop. Time seemed to freeze. Santa turned around, his eyes searching for the source of the noise.

In a flash of quick thinking, Jinx acted. She grabbed a nearby bell and jingled it loudly, creating a cheerful distraction. "Just testing the sleigh bells, Santa!" she called out with a nervous laugh.

Santa, with a twinkle in his eye, smiled and turned back around, none the wiser. Jinx and Jolly let out a silent sigh of relief. With trembling hands but unwavering spirits, they gently placed the last of the special toys into the sack.

As they stepped back, they watched Santa hoist the bag over his shoulder, now complete with the precious gifts they had worked so hard to finish. Santa gave a final nod to his team and climbed onto his sleigh. With a crack of his reindeer's reins, he was off, soaring into the starry Christmas Eve sky.

Jinx and Jolly, standing amidst the fading sound of sleigh bells, knew they had just pulled off the most daring and heartwarming mission of their lives. They had done it – the toys were on their way to bring joy to children around the world.

As Santa's sleigh disappeared into the night, Jinx and Jolly, still awash in adrenaline, retreated into the shadows of the workshop. They watched as the other elves began winding down, unaware of the secret adventure that had just unfolded.

The pair found a quiet spot away from the others, their chests heaving with a mix of exhaustion and exhilaration. They looked at each other, a sense of accomplishment glowing in their eyes. They had done it not just for the children but for the spirit of Christmas itself.

"Thank you," Jinx said softly, her usually stern face breaking into a warm smile. "I couldn't have done this without you."

Jolly, his eyes twinkling with mirth, replied, "And I wouldn't have wanted to do this with anyone but you, Jinx. We make a great team, don't we?"

Jinx, who had always valued precision and order, learned the importance of thinking on her feet and embracing the unexpected. Jolly, with his boundless creativity, understood the value of careful planning and attention to detail. Together, they discovered that embracing each other's strengths led to extraordinary results.

Their friendship, forged in the fires of this Christmas crisis, had grown stronger and deeper.

Later, as the first light of Christmas Day broke over the horizon, the elves gathered to watch the children of the world open their presents, a tradition in Santa's Workshop. Jinx and Jolly, standing side by side, shared a knowing look as they saw the children's faces light up with joy upon receiving the special toys.

Unbeknownst to the other elves, Santa had observed Jinx and Jolly's midnight endeavour. He approached them with a knowing smile. "I saw what you did last night," he said gently. "Your dedication and teamwork embody the true meaning of Christmas. You have my deepest thanks."

The recognition from Santa filled Jinx and Jolly with pride. Their secret mission had not only been successful but had also earned them the respect of the one they admired most.

As the day drew to a close, Jinx and Jolly sat together, looking out at the snowy expanse of the North Pole. They smiled, knowing they had not only preserved the magic of Christmas for children around the world but also strengthened their bond as friends.

Their midnight mission had taught them that every elf, no matter how different, has something valuable to contribute. This newfound understanding and respect for each other's abilities would stay with them, making them an even stronger team in the Christmases to come.

As the Northern Lights danced across the sky, signalling the end of another beautiful Christmas Day, the elves of Santa's

Workshop gathered for a well-deserved celebration. The air was filled with laughter, music, and the sweet aroma of festive treats.

Jinx and Jolly, now known throughout the workshop for their heroic midnight mission, were the guests of honour. Their adventure had become a beloved story, one that would be told for many Christmases to come.

In the midst of the celebration, Santa raised a glass to toast his tireless team. His eyes twinkled as he looked at Jinx and Jolly. "This Christmas," Santa declared, "has taught us an invaluable lesson about the power of friendship, the strength in our differences, and the incredible things we can achieve when we work together."

The elves cheered, their voices ringing out in harmony. They felt a renewed sense of unity and purpose, a reminder that each of them played an essential role in spreading Christmas joy.

As the party continued, Jinx and Jolly stepped outside, gazing up at the starry sky. They thought about the children who were hugging their new toys at that very moment, and their hearts swelled with happiness.

"Next Christmas is going to be even better," Jolly said with a grin.

"Yes, with more planning and maybe a bit of your creativity," Jinx added, smiling.

Hand in hand, they looked out into the night, their thoughts already turning to the wonders of the next Christmas. They knew whatever challenges lay ahead, they would face them together, as a team, as friends.

And so, under the shimmering lights of the North Pole, another magical Christmas came to a close, its spirit kept alive in the hearts of all who believed in the joy and wonder of the season.

The End

The Elves' Twinkling Tour

Reading Time: 15m

In the enchanting realm of the North Pole, where the snow glistens under the winter moon and the air tingles with anticipation for the holiday season, the most magical time of the year was fast approaching. Santa's Workshop, a bustling hive of festive activity, was alive with the sounds of elves busily preparing for Christmas.

At the heart of this festive flurry were two elves, Sparkle and Glint, known throughout the workshop for their love of Christmas lights. Sparkle, with her radiant smile and eyes that twinkled like stars, had a knack for choosing the most dazzling lights. Glint, her ever-cheerful companion, had an uncanny ability to create enchanting light designs that could make even the darkest corners of the world glow with warmth.

One crisp December morning, Santa called Sparkle and Glint to his grand map room, where a massive world map lay sprawled across a table, dotted with twinkling lights representing towns and cities around the globe.

"Sparkle, Glint," Santa began with a twinkle in his eye, "this year, I have a special mission for you." He explained that he wanted to spread extra Christmas cheer to every corner of the world by lighting up towns and cities with magical Christmas lights.

"Our world needs a little extra brightness this year, and who better to bring it than my two brightest elves?" Santa said warmly.

Sparkle and Glint exchanged excited glances. This was their dream come true – a chance to spread joy and light across the world! With a nod and a smile, they eagerly accepted Santa's mission.

As they left the map room, their minds raced with ideas. They would need the brightest, most beautiful lights and, of course, a sprinkle of elvish magic. The task was enormous, but their hearts were full of determination and the spirit of Christmas.

And so, the stage was set for a journey filled with twinkling lights, festive cheer, and a little bit of elvish ingenuity. Sparkle and Glint were about to embark on their Twinkling Tour, a journey that would light up the world and bring smiles to faces everywhere.

Back in the workshop, Sparkle and Glint set to work on their grand mission. Their first task was to gather the most magical Christmas lights and decorations. They searched through shelves lined with boxes of glittering lights, shimmering tinsel, and sparkling ornaments. Each item was carefully selected for its beauty and enchantment.

Sparkle focused on choosing a variety of lights – from twinkling fairy lights to glowing lanterns and colourful LEDs. She knew that each town would need a different type of light to bring out its unique beauty. Glint, meanwhile, gathered tools and gadgets that would help them install the lights in all sorts of places – on tall buildings, around ancient trees, and over bustling market squares.

As they worked, they also brainstormed ideas for each town on their list. "How about cascading lights for the mountain town?" suggested Glint, his eyes gleaming with excitement. "And lanterns that look like floating stars for the seaside village," added Sparkle, her mind alive with visions of their twinkling lights reflecting on the water.

Knowing they would face various challenges, they packed extra supplies for unforeseen situations – weather-proof lights for snowy locales, battery-operated lights for areas with limited electricity, and lightweight decorations that could easily be transported.

The final step in their preparations was mapping their route. They unrolled a large map of the world and plotted their course, starting from small villages and moving to larger towns and cities. Each location was marked with a bright star, symbolising the light they would bring.

Once their sleigh was loaded with boxes of lights and decorations, Sparkle and Glint stood back to admire their work. They were ready to embark on their mission, their hearts filled with excitement and a deep sense of purpose.

Santa, seeing them off, gave them a jolly wave. "Remember, every light you hang is a symbol of hope and joy," he reminded them.

With a final check of their list and a wave to their fellow elves, Sparkle and Glint climbed into their sleigh, their faces beaming with smiles. The reindeer leapt into the sky, and they were off, ready to illuminate the world with the spirit of Christmas.

The first stop on Sparkle and Glint's Twinkling Tour was a bustling town known for its towering skyscrapers and, unfortunately, its incredibly strong winds. As they set up their ladder to start decorating the tallest building, they quickly realised the wind had other plans.

"Just a little gust, nothing to worry about," Glint said confidently as he climbed the ladder with a string of lights. But no sooner had he reached the top than a strong wind whooshed by, causing him to wobble comically on the ladder. Sparkle, at the bottom, tried to steady the ladder but ended up being spun around like a merry-go-round.

Seeing this, Glint had an idea. "Let's turn these winds to our advantage!" he exclaimed. They decided to attach the lights to small kites and let the wind carry them up and around the buildings. It seemed like a perfect solution... until the kites began to fly off with the lights, turning the sky into a bizarre Christmas light show!

The townspeople gathered, laughing and pointing as Sparkle and Glint dashed around, trying to catch the runaway light-kites. It was a chaotic dance of elves, lights, and kites, creating a spectacle that had everyone in stitches.

Finally, with teamwork and a bit of elvish ingenuity, they managed to retrieve the kites and decorate the town, albeit in a more unconventional way. The lights swirled around the buildings in whimsical patterns, creating a unique and unexpectedly beautiful display.

As they moved on to their next destination, Sparkle couldn't help but chuckle. "Well, that was uplifting in more ways than one," she joked, and Glint laughed, his earlier confidence replaced with a more humble grin.

After their windy adventure, Sparkle and Glint arrived at a quaint village blanketed in snow. Their plan was to create a winter wonderland with lights sparkling amidst the snowflakes. However, they hadn't anticipated just how much snow they would have to contend with.

As they began to string lights on the trees, the snow kept piling up, burying their lights faster than they could hang them. "It's like the snow is playing hide and seek with our lights!" chuckled Glint, trying to brush off the thick layers of snow.

Determined not to let a little (or a lot) of snow stop them, they came up with a 'bright' idea. They would use heat-emitting lights that would gently melt the snow around them, keeping the lights visible. It sounded perfect in theory...

But in practice, it turned into a comedy of errors. The heat from the lights caused the snow to melt too quickly, creating little snow slides off the branches. Sparkle, standing under a tree, got a mini avalanche of snow dumped on her head, turning her into a walking, talking snow-elf. Glint couldn't stop laughing, even as he helped to dig her out.

The villagers, amused by the spectacle, joined in to help. Kids started making snow-elves, inspired by Sparkle's new look, while the adults helped adjust the lights to the right temperature.

In the end, the village was transformed into a sparkling wonderland, with lights twinkling through a delicate layer of snow and snow elves dotting the landscape, much to the delight of the local children.

As they left the village, Sparkle, now free of her snowy coating, said with a laugh, "Well, I always wanted to be part of a winter wonderland. Just didn't expect to become part of the scenery!"

Sparkle and Glint's next destination was a small, eco-friendly town known for its commitment to saving energy. Excited to support this green initiative, the elves had brought along their most energy-efficient lights. However, they soon discovered that these lights were a bit too efficient – they were barely visible!

"We need to make these lights brighter without using more energy," Sparkle mused, scratching her head. Glint, always ready with an idea, suggested using mirrors to reflect and amplify the light.

Armed with an array of shiny mirrors, they set to work. But things didn't go quite as planned. Every time they positioned a mirror, it either directed the light into someone's window or, worse, into the eyes of the townspeople. The town quickly turned into a light show of a different kind, with random beams of light crisscrossing the streets, making it look like a disco.

The townspeople, initially puzzled by the sudden light spectacle, soon found the humour in the situation. They started dancing in the streets, turning the light mishap into an impromptu dance party. One resident even brought out a disco ball, adding to the festive atmosphere.

Amidst the laughter and dancing, Sparkle and Glint quickly adjusted their strategy, redirecting the mirrors to create a soft, ambient glow that beautifully lit up the town without wasting energy.

As the impromptu party wound down, the town was aglow with a gentle, eco-friendly light, and the sound of laughter still echoed through the streets. The elves had not only succeeded in their mission but had also sparked a spontaneous celebration.

As they prepared to leave, Glint chuckled and said, "Who knew energy-saving could be so enlightening – and entertaining!" Sparkle nodded, her eyes sparkling with amusement and pride at their accomplishment.

As the last of the Christmas lights twinkled in the eco-friendly town, Sparkle and Glint looked back on their journey with a sense of accomplishment and joy. They had travelled far and wide, facing unexpected challenges and bringing light and laughter to towns and villages around the world.

Their Twinkling Tour had turned into more than just a mission to decorate; it had become a journey of spreading joy, connecting communities, and creating unforgettable memories. From the windy city's light-kite spectacle to the snowy village's snow elves, and finally, the disco dance party in the eco-friendly town, each place had its unique story, all illuminated by the magic of Christmas lights.

As they returned to the North Pole, their sleigh laden with empty boxes and hearts full of stories, the other elves gathered around, eager to hear about their adventures. Sparkle and Glint shared their tales, their eyes shining with excitement. The workshop erupted with laughter and awe at their escapades.

Santa, listening with a wide smile, congratulated them on their successful mission. "You've done more than light up the world; you've spread happiness and brought laughter to so many. You've shown that the true light of Christmas comes from the joy we bring to others," he said warmly.

The elves celebrated their return with a grand feast, the workshop aglow with the very lights they had spread across the globe. The air was filled with cheer, music, and the clinking of cocoa mugs as they toasted to their twinkling adventure.

As the night drew to a close, Sparkle and Glint stood side by side, looking up at the starry sky. They thought about all the people they had met, the challenges they had overcome, and the joy they had spread.

"Until next year," whispered Sparkle, her eyes reflecting the bright constellations above.

"Until next year," echoed Glint, a contented smile on his face.

And with that, another magical Christmas came to an end at the North Pole; its spirit kept alive in the hearts of everyone who had witnessed the elves' twinkling tour.

The End

The Elves' Secret Toy Workshop

Reading Time: 17m

Deep in the heart of the North Pole, where the snow sparkles under the aurora-lit sky and the air is filled with the sweet scent of peppermint, lies a world of wonder and joy - Santa's village. Here, amidst the bustling workshops and jolly laughter of elves, every day is dedicated to the magic of Christmas.

In this enchanting village, two elves, Tinker and Twinkle, were known for their exceptional toy-making skills. Tinker, with his inventive mind and skilled hands, could turn the simplest materials into extraordinary toys. Twinkle, with her artistic flair and eye for detail, added the finishing touches that made each toy a masterpiece.

One crisp, starry night, just weeks before Christmas, Tinker and Twinkle were exploring a seldom-visited part of the village. It was an old, snow-covered path that few had trodden in recent years. Their curiosity led them to a hidden grove, where they discovered an ancient, ivy-covered door set into a snowy hillside.

With a mix of excitement and wonder, they pushed open the creaking door to reveal a long-forgotten workshop. Dusty shelves lined the walls, filled with mysterious tools and faded blueprints of toys they had never seen before. It was like stepping into a treasure trove of the past, a secret haven of toy-making waiting to be brought back to life.

Their eyes sparkling with possibility, Tinker and Twinkle knew they had stumbled upon something special. This hidden workshop was a place where they could create toys unlike any other - toys that would bring surprise and delight to children all over the world.

As they explored this magical workshop, an idea began to form. What if they used this secret place to make unique, one-of-a-kind toys for those children who had sent the most heartwarming letters to Santa?

And so, under the watchful gaze of the twinkling stars, Tinker and Twinkle set the wheels in motion for a secret Christmas project that would soon become the talk of Santa's village.

As Tinker and Twinkle stepped into the dimly lit workshop, they felt a sense of history and mystery enveloping them. The walls were adorned with sketches of toys from generations past, and tools of every shape and size hung neatly in their places, untouched for years.

They gingerly picked up the blueprints, blowing off layers of dust. The designs were for toys of incredible imagination – mechanical dolls that could draw, wooden animals that moved gracefully, and miniature trains with intricate details. These were the toys of old, filled with craftsmanship and charm, waiting to be brought to life once again.

Twinkle's eyes danced with excitement. "These toys... they're like nothing we have in the modern workshop. We could create something truly special for the children!" she exclaimed.

Tinker nodded, already examining the old tools with fascination. "And with a few modern tweaks, we can make them even better!" he said, his mind racing with ideas.

The two elves spent hours in the workshop, planning and experimenting. They decided to focus on a few designs to start with, selecting the ones that would bring the most joy and wonder. Tinker took charge of the mechanical aspects, while Twinkle focused on the aesthetics, ensuring each toy was as beautiful as it was fun.

They worked in secret, sneaking away to the hidden workshop in their spare time. The excitement of their clandestine project gave them a new energy, and they found themselves looking forward to their hidden workshop sessions more than anything else.

As their plans took shape, they realised they would need help to bring these ambitious toys to life in time for Christmas.

They carefully selected a small team of fellow elves who were known for their discretion and skill. Each elf was sworn to secrecy and was thrilled to be part of such a unique project.

Together, they began the delicate task of crafting the toys. The workshop rang with the sounds of sawing, painting, and laughter as the elves worked tirelessly, their hands guided by the joy and anticipation of the children who would receive these magical gifts.

But as they delved deeper into their project, they realised the challenges ahead were greater than they had anticipated. The old designs were complex, and the ancient tools required skills they had yet to master. The task was daunting, but their determination was unwavering.

As the days passed, Tinker, Twinkle, and their team poured their hearts and souls into creating the toys. Each stitch, each brush stroke, and each tiny gear was placed with care and love. They were not just making toys; they were creating memories that would last a lifetime.

In the heart of the hidden workshop, Tinker, Twinkle, and their team of elves faced the true test of their toy-making skills. The ancient designs, though beautiful and intricate, were unlike anything they had worked on before. Each toy required a delicate balance of old-world craftsmanship and new-world innovation.

The first challenge was understanding the old designs. The faded blueprints were written in an archaic elvish script, filled with terms and techniques long forgotten. Tinker spent night after night poring over old toymaking manuals, deciphering the language and methods used by the toy makers of the past.

Meanwhile, Twinkle struggled with the old tools, which were beautiful but unwieldy. She was accustomed to the modern, precision tools of the main workshop and found these historical instruments both fascinating and frustrating. It was a learning curve, requiring patience and practice to master the art of using them.

As the days ticked down to Christmas, the pressure mounted. There were moments of doubt and frustration when a toy wouldn't come together as planned or when a particularly tricky mechanism refused to work. But each challenge was met with determination and a shared commitment to their secret mission.

One of the most memorable challenges came when they attempted to assemble a clockwork horse. The mechanism was so complex that it took several attempts to get it right. During one test run, the horse galloped wildly around the workshop, causing comical chaos as elves ducked and dived to avoid being trampled by the runaway toy.

The laughter that followed the incident lightened their spirits and reminded them of the joy at the heart of their task. Each challenge was an opportunity to learn and grow, and with each setback, their resolve only strengthened.

As they overcame these hurdles, the toys began to take shape. A bear that could paint pictures, a doll that could sing lullabies, a set of building blocks that could assemble themselves - each toy was a testament to the elves' skill and creativity.

The project, kept secret from the rest of Santa's Workshop, became their own little world. A world filled with the spirit of Christmas, where every challenge was an opportunity to bring joy and wonder to a child.

Tinker, Twinkle, and their team worked feverishly to put the finishing touches on their creations. They were determined to make this Christmas one that would be remembered for years to come.

As Christmas Eve drew near, the hidden workshop was a hive of activity. The toys were nearly ready, each one a masterpiece of craftsmanship and love. Tinker, Twinkle, and their team felt a mix of exhaustion and excitement, their hearts buoyed by the thought of the joy these toys would bring.

But just when they thought their secret project was safe, an unforeseen problem threatened to unravel everything. One evening, as they were putting the final touches on a mechanical puppet, a small fire sparked by a short circuit in the toy's wiring. The fire was quickly extinguished, but not before it set off the smoke alarms, sending a loud warning echoing through Santa's village.

Panic ensued in the hidden workshop. "If Santa and the other elves find out, our surprise will be ruined!" Twinkle exclaimed, her eyes wide with worry.

Quick thinking was needed, and Tinker had an idea. He grabbed a handful of magic snow – a special kind of snow that sparkled with a faint glow – and threw it into the air. The snow created a dazzling light display, drawing the attention of the other elves and Santa himself.

"What's this wonderful light show?" Santa asked as he approached the scene, his eyes twinkling with curiosity.
Thinking on their feet, Tinker and Twinkle improvised. "It's a new type of Christmas light display we've been working on," Tinker said with a forced smile.

Santa, delighted by the unexpected spectacle, congratulated them on their innovation. "Just when I think I've seen all the wonders of the North Pole, you surprise me with more!" he chuckled, none the wiser about the true nature of the commotion.

With a sigh of relief, the team watched as Santa and the other elves returned to their preparations, the secret of the hidden workshop safe for now.

After the close call, Tinker, Twinkle, and their team worked with renewed urgency to finish the toys. They knew that they couldn't afford any more mishaps. The clock was ticking, and they had a promise to keep to the children waiting for their special Christmas morning.

The night before Christmas, the hidden workshop was aglow with a warm, festive light. The team of elves, led by Tinker and Twinkle, stood back to admire their handiwork. Before them lay an array of magical toys, each more wondrous than the last, ready to be delivered to children around the world. But first, they had one more task – revealing their secret project to Santa and the rest of the elves. The team quietly transported the toys to the main workshop after everyone had gone to sleep, arranging them for the big reveal.

As dawn broke on Christmas Eve, Santa and the elves awoke to find the workshop transformed. The mysterious, beautifully crafted toys were displayed in the centre of the room, each one with a note detailing the child it was meant for and the story behind its creation.

Santa, surprised and deeply touched, gathered all the elves around. "Who is responsible for this wonderful surprise?" he asked, his eyes sparkling with joy and curiosity.

Tinker and Twinkle stepped forward a little nervously. "We are, Santa," Twinkle said. "And not just us, but this amazing team, too," she added, gesturing to their fellow elves who had helped bring the project to life.

Santa's hearty laugh echoed through the workshop. "You have all outdone yourselves," he said warmly. "These toys are not just gifts; they are works of art, filled with heart and imagination. You've captured the true spirit of Christmas – bringing joy and wonder to children."

The other elves, amazed by the creativity and craftsmanship of the toys, applauded their colleagues. There was a sense of pride and camaraderie in the air, a shared joy in the magic they had all helped create.

As the sleigh was loaded with the special toys, Tinker, Twinkle, and their team felt a surge of fulfilment. They had kept their secret and faced challenges, and now, their dream was about to become a reality.

With a twinkle in his eye, Santa prepared to depart. "These toys will bring so much happiness. Thank you, my clever elves, for reminding us all of the wonders we can create when we put our hearts into it."

And with that, Santa and his reindeer took off into the sky, the sleigh filled with the most unique and heartfelt gifts the North Pole had ever produced.

As the first light of Christmas morning crept across the world, children awoke with bright eyes and eager hearts. Underneath Christmas trees in homes far and wide, the special toys crafted by Tinker, Twinkle, and their team waited to be discovered.

In a cosy house nestled in the snow-covered hills, a little girl unwrapped a mechanical doll that could draw. Her eyes widened with amazement as the doll began to sketch a portrait of her, each stroke filled with precision and care. The girl's laughter and clapping filled the room, her joy echoing like a sweet melody.

Across the ocean, in a bustling city apartment, a boy opened a box to find a set of building blocks that assembled themselves. He watched in awe as the blocks came together to form a miniature castle, towers reaching high, with tiny flags fluttering. His delighted shouts woke the whole household, his excitement infectious.

In another part of the world, a child discovered a clockwork horse that galloped around the room, its mechanism so smooth and life-like that it seemed to be alive. The child's squeals of delight mixed with the gentle clatter of hooves on the floor, creating a symphony of happiness.

Each toy, delivered by Santa, carried with it not just the magic of Christmas but the love and dedication of the elves who had created it. These weren't just gifts; they were embodiments of imagination and wonder, connecting the hearts of the elves to the hearts of children around the globe.

As the day unfolded, letters of gratitude and stories of joy began to flood into Santa's Workshop. Children wrote of their awe and wonder at the unique toys they had received, their words a testament to the impact of the elves' hard work.

Back at the North Pole, Tinker, Twinkle, and their team read each letter with teary eyes and full hearts. They had hoped to make a difference, to bring a special kind of joy to Christmas, but they hadn't anticipated the overwhelming wave of happiness their toys would bring.

Santa, watching his elves bask in the gratitude and love flowing in from all corners of the world, felt a deep sense of pride. His workshop had not just created toys; it had created memories that would last a lifetime.

As the sun set on a memorable Christmas Day, the North Pole was alive with a festive glow. The elves gathered in Santa's Workshop, sharing stories and laughter, the air filled with a sense of accomplishment and joy.

Santa called Tinker, Twinkle, and their team to the centre of the workshop. "Your secret toy workshop has not only created extraordinary gifts but has also brought a new kind of magic to Christmas," Santa said, his voice warm with gratitude. "You've shown us all the beauty of innovation and the power of a dream."

It was decided that the hidden workshop would become a new tradition at the North Pole. Each year, a team of elves would be chosen to create special, one-of-a-kind toys for children around the world. Tinker and Twinkle were appointed as the first guardians of this tradition, a role they accepted with humble smiles and sparkling eyes.

The story of the secret toy workshop spread far and wide, inspiring elves and children alike. It became a symbol of the endless possibilities that come with imagination, creativity, and a desire to bring happiness to others.

Tinker and Twinkle often visited the hidden workshop, now a place of endless inspiration and joy. They would stand amidst the tools and toys, a reminder of the adventure that had brought so much happiness.

And so, as the Northern Lights danced in the sky above, another Christmas season came to a close at the North Pole. The elves' secret toy workshop had become a cherished part of the holiday, a testament to the belief that the greatest gifts come from the heart.

In homes around the world, the special toys stood as a reminder of the magic of Christmas, of the love and care that had gone into their creation. And in the hearts of children, the wonder and joy of that Christmas morning would remain a treasured memory for years to come.

The End

Printed in Great Britain
by Amazon

34205411R00026